The TEACHER Who COULD NOT COUNT

Hess

by Craig McKee and Margaret Holland

illustrated by Steve Romney

The Teacher Who Could Not Count is one of a series of Predictable Read Together Books edited by Dr. Margaret Holland. Books in this series are designed to help young children begin to read naturally and easily. See back cover for additional information.

Published by Willowisp Press®, Inc., 401 E. Wilson Bridge Road, Worthington, Ohio 43085

Printed in the United States of America   10 9 8 7 6   ISBN 0-87406-125-3

Once there was a teacher who could not count.
On the first day of school,
the children came to their teacher's classroom.

There weren't enough chairs for all the children.

The teacher asked for more chairs.
Then there were too many chairs.

Sometimes the children had too many books.
Sometimes they didn't have enough books.

Sometimes they had too many lunches.
Sometimes they didn't have enough lunches.

"Can't you count?" the principal asked.
The teacher didn't answer.

The class took a trip to the zoo.

Twenty-nine children went to the zoo.

Only twenty-six children came back from the zoo.

The principal had to go to the zoo to find the three missing children.

"If you can't count, you can't teach,"
the principal told the teacher.

All the children were sad. They liked their teacher very much.
"We must help our teacher learn to count," said Tommy.
"Yes! Yes!" said the children.

They tried to help their teacher count the chairs.
They tried to help her count the books.

They tried to help her count the lunches.
But the teacher couldn't count.
The children wrote the numbers on the blackboard.
But their teacher still couldn't count.

"What else can we do?" asked Fred.
"Let's all close our eyes and think," said Eileen.

So they all closed their eyes and thought and thought.

"I know," said Olga. "We could write the numbers on her arm."
"We could bake number cookies," said Frank.
"Or we could be the numbers ourselves," said Steve.
"Let's be the numbers!" cried Tina.

Hurray! Let's be numbers!" said the children.

I'll be 1," said Olga.

"I'll be 2," said Tommy.

"I'll be 3," said Tina.

"I can be 5," said Fred.

"I can be 4," said Frank.

"And I can be 6," said Su

"I'm 7!" said Steve.

"And I'm 9," laughed Nancy.

"I'm 8!" shouted Eileen.

"Look at us, teacher.
We can help you count," cried the children.

"Now I see," said the teacher.
"Thank you."

So the teacher counted the children.
Then she counted the chairs.
Then she counted the books.

"Hurray!" said all the children.
"Hurray!" said the principal.
"OUR TEACHER CAN COUNT